With love to my beautiful children,
Zoe, Yasmin, Jacob and Dylan

First published in 2018 by Child's Play (International) Ltd
Ashworth Road, Bridgemead, Swindon SN5 7YD, UK

Published in USA by Child's Play Inc
250 Minot Avenue, Auburn, Maine 04210

Distributed in Australia by Child's Play Australia Pty Ltd
Unit 10/20 Narabang Way, Belrose, Sydney, NSW 2085

ISBN 978-1-78628-202-6
CPL130318CPL06182026

Printed in Shenzhen, China

1 3 5 7 9 10 8 6 4 2

A catalogue record of this book
is available from the British Library

www.childs-play.com

GENTLY, BENTLEY!

Caragh Buxton

This is a picture of
Bentley Oliver Anthony Brown.

He's five and a half years old.
He's a bright little spark, very tough and very bold.

Bentley is full of energy
and gets excited easily...

...and sometimes this can get him into trouble.

There was the time Bentley had eggs for breakfast.

He was in such a rush that
the yolk went everywhere!

When it was time
to go to school...

Bentley ran down the stairs
with such thunderous haste...

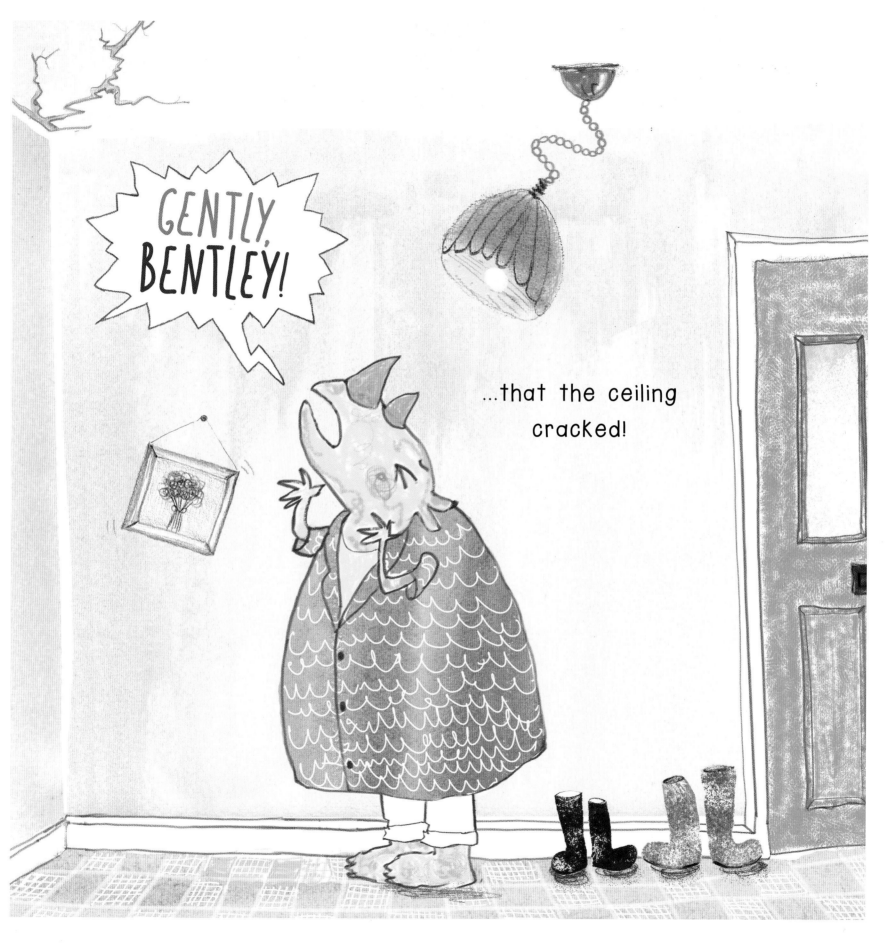

It was the same story at school.

square
triangle
circle

Bentley was in such a rush
to fetch his pencils and books...

...that it was difficult for him to hold on to them all.

Everything just went flying!

During break he loved to play...

Chase

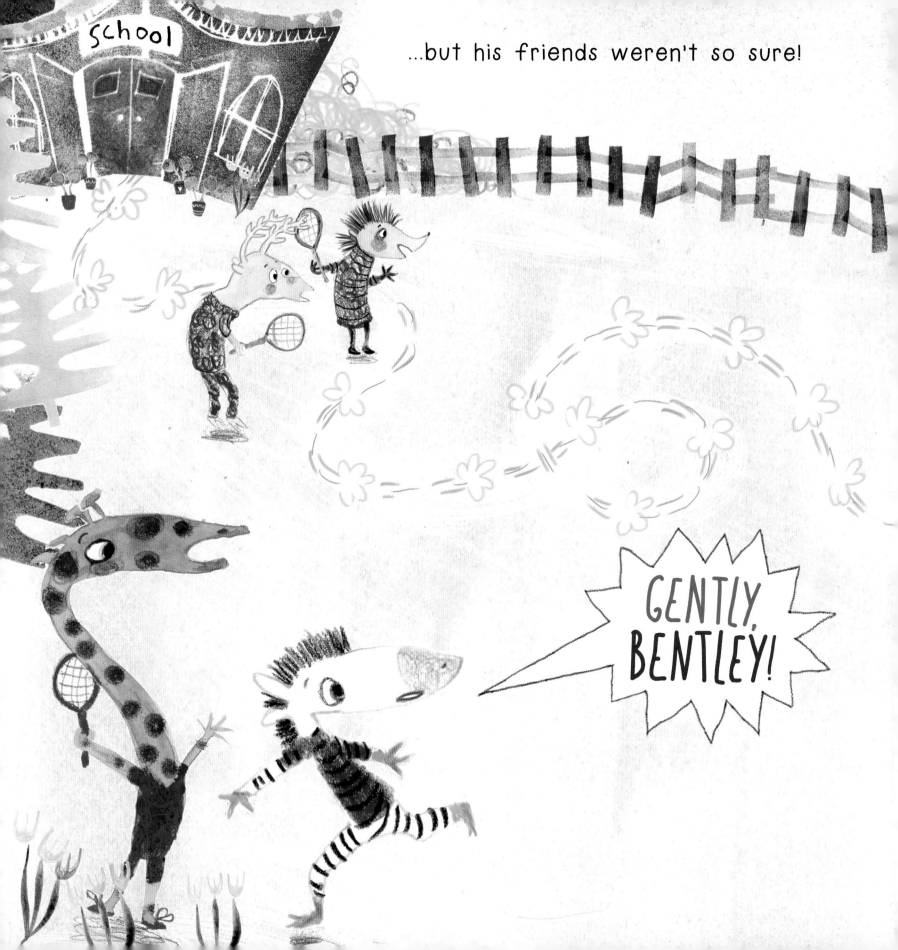

...but his friends weren't so sure!

GENTLY, BENTLEY!

On the way home,
Bentley wanted
to see the ducks...

...but the ducks had other ideas!

The wall posters read:

E is for Elephant

L is for Lion

Rhino Tales

Later that night,
Bentley spotted the baby
sleeping in the cot.

Baby was very quiet.

And this time Bentley was...

...very, very gentle!